CONTENTS

Meet Your Pokémon Pals!	6	The Race Is On!	58
New Character Profiles	8	New Character Profiles	60
Evolution Confusion	12	In the Knicker of Time	64
Who's That Pokémon?	13	New Character Profiles	82
Get the Show on the Road	14	Which Way, May?	86
New Character Profiles	32	Pikachu's Pals	87
Pokémon Artist	36	A Poached Ego	88
There's No Place Like Hoenn	38	New Character Profiles	106
What's Your Team?	56	Answers	110

POKÉMON ADVANCED ™

Pedigree®

Published by Pedigree Books Limited
Beech Hill House, Walnut Gardens, Exeter, Devon EX4 4DH.

E-mail books@pedigreegroup.co.uk

Published 2004

£7.99

MEET YOUR POKéMON PALS

PIKACHU™

Pikachu is an electric-type Pokémon and Ash's best friend. Together they face new adventures and challenges in the Hoenn Region. Pikachu is always Ash's number one choice!

ASH™

Ash is a young Pokémon trainer, driven by passion and determination to pursue his dream of becoming the ultimate Pokémon Master.

BROCK™

Brock is a skilful Pokémon breeder and a gourmet cook! His patience balances out Ash's impulsiveness.

MAY™

May is just starting out on her journey to become a Pokémon trainer with her first Pokémon, Torchic. She has a passion for life – most of all she loves travelling on the open road!

MAX™

May's younger brother knows all the facts about Pokémon, but he still has to learn how to put his knowledge into practice.

TEAM ROCKET™

Jessie, James and Meowth are always trying (and failing!) to catch Pikachu for their boss, Giovanni.

TEAM MAGMA™

One of the world's most evil syndicates, Team Magma is a much bigger threat than the bumbling Team Rocket. Ash had better beware!

Before you can catch a Pokémon you will need a Poké Ball to put it in.

The Pokédex is full of valuable information to help you train your Pokémon.

THE STORY SO FAR...

Ash Ketchum, a young Pokémon trainer from Pallet Town, has set out to become the world's greatest Pokémon Master. By his side is his faithful Pokémon Pikachu, who has been with him since the beginning.

Ash has finished the Johto League Silver Conference with honours. Hoping that the Hoenn gym circuit will be the league where he finally rises to first place, Ash is anxious to begin his journey with Pikachu in this new land.

1 TREECKO

Category: Wood Gecko
Type: Grass
Attacks: Pound, Leer, Absorb, Quick Attack, Pursuit, Screech, Mega Drain, Agility, Slam, Detect, Giga Drain
Evolution: >Grovyle >Sceptile
Height: 0.5m/1'8"
Weight: 5kg/11lb

2 GROVYLE

Category: Wood Gecko
Type: Grass
Attacks: Pound, Leer, Absorb, Quick Attack, Fury Cutter, Pursuit, Screech, Leaf Blade, Agility, Slam, Detect, False Swipe
Evolution: >Sceptile
Height: 0.9m/2'11"
Weight: 21.6kg/48lb

3 SCEPTILE

Category: Forest
Type: Grass
Attacks: Pound, Leer, Absorb, Quick Attack, Fury Cutter, Pursuit, Screech, Leaf Blade, Agility, Slam, Detect, False Swipe
Evolution: None
Height: 1.7m/5'7"
Weight: 52.2kg/115lb

4 TORCHIC

Category: Chick
Type: Fire
Attacks: Scratch, Growl, Focus Energy, Ember, Peck, Sand Attack, Fire Spin, Quick Attack, Slash, Mirror Move, Flamethrower
Evolution: >Combusken> Blaziken
Height: 0.4m/1'4"
Weight: 2.5kg/6lb

5 COMBUSKEN

Category: Young Fowl
Type: Fire/Fighting
Attacks: Scratch, Growl, Focus Energy, Ember, Double Kick, Peck, Sand Attack, Bulk Up, Quick Attack, Slash, Mirror Move, Sky Uppercut
Evolution: >Blaziken
Height: 0.9m/2'11'
Weight: 19.5kg/43lb

6 BLAZIKEN

Category: Blaze
Type: Fire/Fighting
Attacks: Fire Punch, Scratch, Growl, Focus Energy, Ember, Double Kick, Peck, Sand Attack, Bulk Up, Quick Attack, Blaze Kick, Slash, Mirror Move, Sky Uppercut
Evolution: None
Height: 1.9m/6'3"
Weight: 52kg/115lb

7 MUDKIP

Category: Mud Fish
Type: Water
Attacks: Tackle, Growl, Mud Slap, Water Gun, Bide, Foresight, Mud Sport, Take Down, Whirlpool, Protect, Hydro Pump, Endeavour
Evolution: >Marshtomp>Swampert
Height: 0.4m/1'4"
Weight: 7.6kg/17lb

8 MARSHTOMP

Category: Mud Fish
Type: Water/Ground
Attacks: Tackle, Growl, Mudslap, Water Gun, Bide, Mud Shot, Foresight, Mud Sport, Take Down, Muddy Water, Protect, Earthquake, Endeavour
Evolution: >Swampert
Height: 0.7m/2'4"
Weight: 28kg/62lb

9 SWAMPERT

Category: Mud Fish
Type: Water/Ground
Attacks: Tackle, Growl, Mudslap, Water Gun, Bide, Mud Shot, Foresight, Mud Sport, Take Down, Muddy Water, Protect, Earthquake, Endeavour
Evolution: None
Height: 1.5m/4'11"
Weight: 81.9kg/181lb

10 POOCHYENA

Category: Bite
Type: Dark
Attacks: Tackle, Howl, Sand Attack, Bite, Odour Sleuth, Roar, Swagger, Scary Face, Take Down, Taunt, Crunch, Thief
Evolution: >Mightyena
Height: 0.5m/1'8"
Weight: 13.6kg/30lb

11 MIGHTYENA

Category: Bite
Type: Dark
Attacks: Tackle, Howl, Sand Attack, Bite, Odour Sleuth, Roar, Swagger, Scary Face, Take Down, Taunt, Crunch, Thief
Evolution: None
Height: 1m/3'3"
Weight: 37kg/82lb

12 ZIGZAGOON

Category: Tinyraccoon
Type: Normal
Attacks: Tackle, Growl, Tail Whip, Headbutt, Sand Attack, Odour Sleuth, Mud Sport, Pin Missile, Covet, Flail, Rest, Belly Drum
Evolution: >Linoone
Height: 0.4m/1'4"
Weight: 17.5kg/39lb

13 LINOONE

Category: Rushing
Type: Normal
Attacks: Tackle, Growl, Tail Whip, Headbutt, Sand Attack, Odour Sleuth, Mud Sport, Fury Swipes, Covet, Slash, Rest, Belly Drum
Evolution: None
Height: 0.5m/1'8"
Weight: 32.5kg/72lb

14 WURMPLE

Category: Worm
Type: Bug
Attacks: Tackle, String Shot, Poison Sting
Evolution: >Silcoon >Beautifly OR >Cascoon>Dustox
Height: 0.3m/1'0"
Weight: 3.6kg/8lb

15 SILCOON

Category: Cocoon
Type: Bug
Attacks: Harden
Evolution: >Beautifly
Height: 0.6m/2'0"
Weight: 10kg/22lb

16 BEAUTIFLY

Category: Butterfly
Type: Bug/Flying
Attacks: Absorb, Gust, Stun Spore, Morning Sun, Mega Drain, Whirlwind, Giga Drain, Attract, Silver Wind
Evolution: None
Height: 1m/3'3"
Weight: 28.4kg/63lb

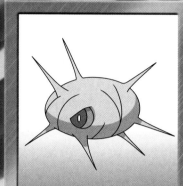

17 CASCOON

Category: Cocoon
Type: Bug
Attacks: Harden
Evolution: >Dustox
Height: 0.7m/2'4"
Weight: 11.5kg/25lb

18 DUSTOX

Category: Toxic Moth
Type: Bug/Poison
Attacks: Confusion, Gust, Protect, Moonlight, Psybeam, Whirlwind, Light Screen, Toxic, Silver Wind
Evolution: None
Height: 1.2m/3'11"
Weight: 31.6kg/70lb

19 LOTAD

Category: Water Weed
Type: Water/Grass
Attacks: Astonish, Growl, Absorb, Nature Power, Mist, Rain Dance, Mega Drain
Evolution: >Lombre >Ludicolo
Height: 0.5m/1'8"
Weight: 2.6kg/6lb

20 LOMBRE

Category: Jolly
Type: Water/Grass
Attacks: Astonish, Growl, Absorb, Nature Power, Fake Out, Fury Swipes, Water Sport, Thief, Uproar, Hydro Pump
Evolution: >Ludicolo
Height: 1.2m/3'11"
Weight: 32.5kg/72lb

21 LUDICOLO

Category: Carefree
Type: Water/Grass
Attacks: Astonish, Growl, Absorb, Nature Power
Evolution: None
Height: 1.5m/4'11"
Weight: 55kg/121lb

26 SWELLOW

Category: Swallow
Type: Normal/Flying
Attacks: Peck, Growl, Focus Energy, Quick Attack, Wing Attack, Double Team, Endeavour, Aerial Ace, Agility
Evolution: None
Height: 0.7m/2'4"
Weight: 19.8kg/44lb

22 SEEDOT

Category: Acorn
Type: Grass
Attacks: Bide, Harden, Growth, Nature Power, Synthesis, Sunny Day, Explosion
Evolution: >Nuzleaf >Shiftry
Height: 0.5m/1'8"
Weight: 4kg/9lb

27 WINGULL

Category: Seagull
Type: Water/Flying
Attacks: Growl, Water Gun, Supersonic, Wing Attack, Mist, Quick Attack, Pursuit, Agility
Evolution: >Pelipper
Height: 0.6m/2'0"
Weight: 9.5kg/21lb

23 NUZLEAF

Category: Wily
Type: Grass/Dark
Attacks: Pound, Harden, Growth, Nature Power, Fake Out, Torment, Faint Attack, Razor Wind, Swagger, Extrasensory
Evolution: >Shiftry
Height: 1m/3'3"
Weight: 28kg/62lb

28 PELIPPER

Category: Water Bird
Type: Water/Flying
Attacks: Growl, Water Gun, Water Sport, Wing Attack, Supersonic, Mist, Protect, Stockpile, Swallow, Spit Up, Hydro Pump
Evolution: None
Height: 1.2m/3'11"
Weight: 28kg/62lb

24 SHIFTRY

Category: Wicked
Type: Grass/Dark
Attacks: Pound, Harden, Growth, Nature Power
Evolution: None
Height: 1.3m/4'3"
Weight: 59.6kg/131lb

29 RALTS

Category: Feeling
Type: Psychic
Attacks: Growl, Confusion, Double Team, Teleport, Calm Mind, Psychic, Imprison, Future Sight, Hypnosis, Dream Eater
Evolution: >Kirlia >Gardevoir
Height: 0.4m/1'4"
Weight: 6.6kg/15lb

25 TAILLOW

Category: Tinyswallow
Type: Normal/Flying
Attacks: Peck, Growl, Focus Energy, Quick Attack, Wing Attack, Double Team, Endeavour, Aerial Ace, Agility
Evolution: >Swellow
Height: 0.3m/1'0"
Weight: 2.3kg/5lb

30 KIRLIA

Category: Emotion
Type: Psychic
Attacks: Growl, Confusion, Double Team, Teleport, Calm Mind, Psychic, Imprison, Future Sight, Hypnosis, Dream Eater
Evolution: >Gardevoir
Height: 0.8m/2'7"
Weight: 20.2kg/45lb

31 GARDEVOIR

Category: Embrace
Type: Psychic
Attacks: Growl, Confusion, Double Team, Teleport, Calm Mind, Psychic, Imprison, Future Sight, Hypnosis, Dream Eater
Evolution: None
Height: 1.6m/5'3"
Weight: 48.4kg/107lb

32 SURSKIT

Category: Pond Skater
Type: Bug/Water
Attacks: Bubble, Quick Attack, Sweet Scent, Water Sport, Bubble Beam, Agility, Mist, Haze
Evolution: >Masquerain
Height: 0.5m/1'8"
Weight: 1.7kg/4lb

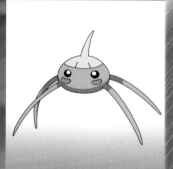

33 MASQUERAIN

Category: Eyeball
Type: Bug/Flying
Attacks: Bubble, Quick Attack, Sweet Scent, Water Sport, Gust, Scary Face, Stun Spore, Silver Wind, Whirlwind
Evolution: None
Height: 0.8m/2'7"
Weight: 3.6kg/8lb

34 SHROOMISH

Category: Mushroom
Type: Grass
Attacks: Absorb, Tackle, Stun Spore, Leech Seed, Mega Drain, Headbutt, Poisonpowder, Growth, Giga Drain, Spore
Evolution: >Breloom
Height: 0.4m/1'4"
Weight: 4.5kg/10lb

35 BRELOOM

Category: Mushroom
Type: Grass/Fighting
Attacks: Absorb, Tackle, Stun Spore, Leech Seed, Mega Drain, Headbutt, Mach Punch, Counter, Sky Uppercut, Mind Reader, Dynamicpunch
Evolution: None
Height: 1.2m/3'11"
Weight: 39.2kg/86lb

36 SLAKOTH

Category: Slacker
Type: Normal
Attacks: Scratch, Yawn, Encore, Slack Off, Faint Attack, Amnesia, Covet, Counter, Flail
Evolution: >Vigoroth >Slaking
Height: 0.8m/2'7"
Weight: 24kg/53lb

37 VIGOROTH

Category: Wild Monkey
Type: Normal
Attacks: Scratch, Focus Energy, Encore, Uproar, Fury Swipes, Endure, Slash, Counter, Focus Punch, Reversal
Evolution: >Slaking
Height: 1.4m/4'7"
Weight: 46.5kg/103lb

38 SLAKING

Category: Lazy
Type: Normal
Attacks: Scratch, Yawn, Encore, Slack Off, Faint Attack, Amnesia, Covet, Swagger, Counter, Flail
Evolution: None
Height: 2m/6'7"
Weight: 130.5kg/288lb

39 ABRA

Category: PSI
Type: Psychic
Attacks: Teleport
Evolution: >Kadabra >Alakazam
Height: 0.9m/2'11"
Weight: 19.5kg/43lb

40 KADABRA

Category: PSI
Type: Psychic
Attacks: Teleport, Kinesis, Confusion, Disable, Psybeam, Reflect, Recover, Future Sight, Role Play, Psychic, Trick
Evolution: >Alakazam
Height: 1.3m/4'3"
Weight: 56.5kg/125lb

EVOLUTION CONFUSION

Team Rocket is a bit confused (as usual)! Five of their new Pokémon have evolved, but they don't recognise them! Follow the wiggly lines with your finger to find out what each Pokémon has evolved into.

WHO'S THAT POKéMON?

Can you help Ash match these Pokémon to their shadows?
Draw a line to connect each Pokémon to the correct shadow.

a

1

b

2

c

3

d

e

4

f

5

6

Answers: a-3 b-4 c-6 d-5 e-2 f-1

Answers: a-3   b-4   c-6   d-5   e-2   f-1

13

GET THE SHOW ON THE ROAD!

`Ten-year-old May was travelling to Littleroot Town to meet a friend of her father's. Professor Birch would give her a Beginner's Pokémon, so she could begin her journey as a Pokémon trainer. But May didn't care about being a Pokémon trainer. She just wanted to travel and see new places.

Suddenly a Duskull Pokémon appeared next to May. It gave her such a scare that she crashed her bike into a tree!

"Owww!" she groaned. "I really don't like Pokémon!" Then she saw the beautiful bay of Littleroot Town, where a ferry was chugging in. "But the travelling – I just love it!"

Down on the ferry, Ash was anxiously cradling
Pikachu in his arms.
"Just try to rest, Pikachu," he said.
"As soon as we dock I'll take you to the Pokémon Centre."
Ash had finished the Johto League Silver Conference with honours, and was
going to the Hoenn region to continue his journey. But Pikachu was ill, sparking
with electricity, and now Ash could think about nothing except helping his friend.
On the other side of the ferry, Team Rocket was leaning on the railings.
"Ladies and Gentlemen," said the captain, "welcome to Littleroot Town."

Ash hurried into Littleroot Town, only to find that there wasn't a Pokémon Centre! Then he had an idea. Professor Birch, a Pokémon expert, had a laboratory nearby. Ash called the laboratory and Joshua, Professor Birch's assistant, promised that the professor would come immediately. When Professor Birch saw Pikachu, he knew that it was serious.

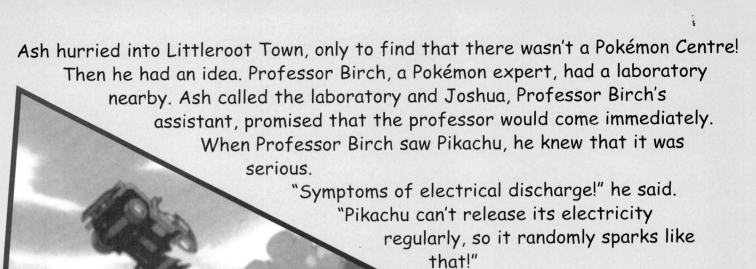

"Symptoms of electrical discharge!" he said. "Pikachu can't release its electricity regularly, so it randomly sparks like that!"

Pikachu started to struggle.

"The high fever is confusing it!" he said grimly. "We've got to get it to the lab immediately!"

At the laboratory, Professor Birch
connected Pikachu to a large machine.
"This is a device that will take away all Pikachu's trapped
electricity," explained Professor Birch.
Ash watched anxiously as Pikachu sparked more and more, but the professor
kept going.

Then the machine began to shudder and smoke!
"It's too much!" yelled Joshua. "It won't hold!"
BOOM!!
The machine exploded! Before Ash could do anything, the frightened
Pikachu jumped out of the window and headed for the mountains!

The professor grabbed three Poké Balls and dashed after Pikachu, Ash close behind him.
"When May gets here, just tell her to wait!" Professor Birch called to Joshua.

While Ash and the professor were searching desperately for Pikachu, May arrived at the laboratory.

"I'm looking for Professor Birch," she told Joshua.

"He had an emergency in the mountains," explained Joshua, "But he asked that you wait for him here."

"Oh! Then I'll go and find him," said May cheerfully. She jumped back on her bike and pedalled away.

"Wait!" cried Joshua. "Hold on!"

"I've never been much good at waiting!" called May.

Team Rocket was watching from their hiding place and saw Ash and Professor Birch run after Pikachu. They dashed off in pursuit.

Ash and the professor split up to search. But Professor Birch fell down a steep hill, dropping his bag! He landed next to a sleeping Poochyena, who turned on him angrily. Two more Poochyena appeared and the professor backed away.

"Can't we discuss this?" he stammered as they sprang at him. "Help!"

He had just climbed a tall tree when May appeared.
"May!" said the professor thankfully. "Great timing! Grab any of the Poké Balls in that bag – and hurry!"

May picked one at random. It was a Mudkip!
"Now what should I do?" she asked.
"Just say 'use Water Gun now'!" cried
Professor Birch.
"Use Water Gun!" said May. The Mudkip
soaked her with water!
"Mudkip! This way!" yelled the professor.
"Use Water Gun on the Poochyena!"
At last Mudkip attacked the Poochyena,
who ran away as fast as they could!
Professor Birch returned Mudkip to the
Poké Ball.

"Professor, what were you doing in that tree?" asked May.
Before he could explain, they saw a powerful electrical charge close by.
"Pikachu's electrical build up is reaching critical mass!" said Professor Birch. "It might explode!"
They followed the crackling electricity and found Ash with Pikachu.
"Ash, get away!" yelled Professor Birch. "Pikachu could explode at any moment!"
"But I've gotta help!" cried Ash. Suddenly Professor Birch gave a cry.
"What's that?"
A huge machine had appeared, and at the controls was...

"Team Rocket!" said Ash. "They keep trying to catch Pikachu!"
"This machine'll beat Pikachu at its own game," chuckled Meowth. "No matter how high its volts go, the machine'll absorb them!"
A metal pincer shot out of the machine and grabbed Pikachu before Ash could do anything! With a crackle, the machine started to drain Pikachu of his electricity! Electricity was crackling over the machine and sparking off in all directions.
"Pikachu!" yelled Ash.

"Pikachu's output is incredible!" gasped Professor Birch. Pikachu gave another burst of power and destroyed May's bike with a dart of electricity.
"My bike's barbequed!" cried May.

Inside the machine, Team Rocket was starting to get worried.
"Can you smell something burning?" asked Jessie. "I think it's us!"
BOOM!
The machine couldn't handle Pikachu's power! It exploded, sending Team Rocket blasting into the sky! Ash rushed over to where Pikachu lay on the ground.
"Let's get it to my lab as quickly as possible," said Professor Birch.

Back at the laboratory, Professor Birch examined Pikachu.
"Pikachu's electricity has reached normal levels," said Joshua.
"That machine must have absorbed all Pikachu's unneeded electricity,"
said Professor Birch. "By tomorrow, it will be as good as new."

Ash looked relieved and May smiled at him.
"I should introduce myself," she said.
"I'm May."
"I'm Ash Ketchum from Pallet Town," he replied, shaking hands.

"Well, May," said Professor Birch. "Are you ready to choose your first Pokémon?" He put three Poké Balls in front of her. "These contain three Beginner Pokémon," he explained. "First up... Treecko!"

"Cool!" said Ash.

"Creepy!" shivered May.

"The next one is... Mudkip!"

"That Mudkip wouldn't do a single thing I asked it to!" said May.

"How could that little guy cause trouble?" laughed Ash.

"Next I'd like you to meet... Torchic!" finished Professor Birch.

"Awesome!" said Ash.

"This one's not so bad," admitted May. "I choose Torchic!"

"Take that Pokédex and those Poké Balls too," said Professor Birch. "If you work hard you could become an even better Pokémon trainer than your father!"

"I'd give up Pokémon any day of the week for a trip around the world," thought May, sadly.

Next morning, it was time for Ash and May to leave.
"You both have to register for the Hoenn League at the nearest
Pokémon Centre," Professor Birch told them. "The nearest one is in
Oldale Town."
"Walking all that way alone makes me nervous," said May. "And my bike's
destroyed... Hey! Why don't we all go together? I know the way!"

Ash hesitated for a moment, and then grinned.
"Okay! We'll go together!"
"Look after each other!" said Professor Birch.
"We will," promised Ash as they set off and waved goodbye.
"Thanks for all your help!"

41 ALAKAZAM

Category: PSI
Type: Psychic
Attacks: Teleport, Kinesis, Confusion, Disable, Psybeam, Reflect, Recover, Future Sight, Calm Mind, Psychic, Trick
Evolution: None
Height: 1.5m/4'11"
Weight: 48kg/106lb

46 LOUDRED

Category: Big Voice
Type: Normal
Attacks: Pound, Uproar, Astonish, Howl, Supersonic, Stomp, Screech, Roar, Rest, Sleep Talk, Hyper Voice
Evolution: >Exploud
Height: 1m/3'3"
Weight: 40.5kg/89lb

42 NINCADA

Category: Trainee
Type: Bug/Ground
Attacks: Scratch, Harden, Leech Life, Sand Attack, Fury Swipes, Mind Reader, False Swipe, Mud Slap, Metal Claw, Dig
Evolution: >Ninjask >Shedinja
Height: 0.5m/1'8"
Weight: 5.5kg/12lb

47 EXPLOUD

Category: Loud Noise
Type: Normal
Attacks: Pound, Uproar, Astonish, Howl, Supersonic, Stomp, Screech, Hyper Beam, Roar, Rest, Sleep Talk, Hyper Voice
Evolution: None
Height: 1.5m/4'11"
Weight: 84kg/185lb

43 NINJASK

Category: Ninja
Type: Bug/Flying
Attacks: Scratch, Harden, Leech Life, Sand Attack, Fury Swipes, Mind Reader, Double Team, Fury Cutter, Screech, Swords Dance, Slash, Agility, Baton Pass
Evolution: >Shedinja
Height: 0.8m/2'7"
Weight: 12kg/26lb

48 MAKUHITA

Category: Guts
Type: Fighting
Attacks: Tackle, Focus Energy, Sand Attack, Arm Thrust, Vital Throw, Fake Out, Whirlwind, Knock Off, Smellingsalt, Belly Drum, Endure, Seismic Toss, Reversal
Evolution: >Hariyama
Height: 1m/3'3"
Weight: 86.4kg/191lb

44 SHEDINJA

Category: Shed
Type: Bug/Ghost
Attacks: Scratch, Harden, Leech Life, Sand Attack, Fury Swipes, Mind Reader, Spite, Confuse Ray, Shadow Ball, Grudge
Evolution: None
Height: 0.8m/2'7"
Weight: 1.2kg/3lb

49 HARIYAMA

Category: Arm Thrust
Type: Fighting
Attacks: Tackle, Focus Energy, Sand Attack, Arm Thrust, Vital Throw, Fake Out, Whirlwind, Knock Off, Smellingsalt, Belly Drum, Endure, Seismic Toss, Reversal
Evolution: None
Height: 2.3m/7'7"
Weight: 253.8kg/560lb

45 WHISMUR

Category: Whisper
Type: Normal
Attacks: Pound, Uproar, Astonish, Howl, Supersonic, Stomp, Screech, Roar, Rest, Sleep Talk, Hyper Voice
Evolution: >Loudred >Exploud
Height: 0.6m/2'0"
Weight: 16.3kg/36lb

50 GOLDEEN

Category: Goldfish
Type: Water
Attacks: Peck, Tail Whip, Water Sport, Supersonic, Horn Attack, Flail, Fury Attack, Waterfall, Horn Drill, Agility
Evolution: >Seaking
Height: 0.6m/2'0"
Weight: 15kg/33lb

51 SEAKING

Category: Goldfish
Type: Water
Attacks: Peck, Tail Whip, Water Sport, Supersonic, Horn Attack, Flail, Fury Attack, Waterfall, Horn Drill, Agility
Evolution: None
Height: 1.3m/4'3"
Weight: 39kg/86lb

52 MAGIKARP

Category: Fish
Type: Water
Attacks: Splash, Tackle, Flail
Evolution: >Gyarados
Height: 0.9m/2'11"
Weight: 10kg/22lb

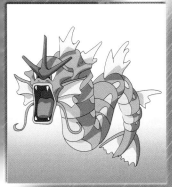

53 GYARADOS

Category: Atrocious
Type: Water/Flying
Attacks: Thrash, Bite, Dragon Rage, Leer, Twister, Hydro Pump, Rain Dance, Dragon Dance, Hyper Beam
Evolution: None
Height: 6.5m/21'4"
Weight: 235kg/518lb

54 AZURILL

Category: Polka Dot
Type: Normal
Attacks: Splash, Charm, Tail Whip, Bubble, Slam, Water Gun
Evolution: >Marill >Azumarill
Height: 0.2m/0'8"
Weight: 2kg/4lb

55 MARILL

Category: Aqua Mouse
Type: Water
Attacks: Tackle, Defence Curl, Tail Whip, Water Gun, Rollout, Bubblebeam, Double Edge, Rain Dance, Hydro Pump
Evolution: >Azumarill
Height: 0.4m/1'4"
Weight: 8.5kg/19lb

56 AZUMARILL

Category: Aqua Rabbit
Type: Water
Attacks: Tackle, Defence Curl, Tail Whip, Water Gun, Rollout, Bubblebeam, Double Edge, Rain Dance, Hydro Pump
Evolution: None
Height: 0.8m/2'7"
Weight: 28.5kg/63lb

57 GEODUDE

Category: Rock
Type: Rock/Ground
Attacks: Tackle, Defence Curl, Mud Sport, Rock Throw, Magnitude, Selfdestruct, Rollout, Rock Blast, Earthquake, Explosion, Double Edge
Evolution: >Graveler >Golem
Height: 0.4m/1'4"
Weight: 20kg/44lb

58 GRAVELER

Category: Rock
Type: Rock/Ground
Attacks: Tackle, Defence Curl, Mud Sport, Rock Throw, Magnitude, Selfdestruct, Rollout, Rock Blast, Earthquake, Explosion, Double Edge
Evolution: >Golem
Height: 1m/3'3"
Weight: 105kg/232lb

59 GOLEM

Category: Megaton
Type: Rock/Ground
Attacks: Tackle, Defence Curl, Mud Sport, Rock Throw, Magnitude, Selfdestruct, Rollout, Rock Blast, Earthquake, Explosion, Double Edge
Evolution: None
Height: 1.4m/4'7"
Weight: 300kg/662lb

60 NOSEPASS

Category: Compass
Type: Rock
Attacks: Tackle, Harden, Rock Throw, Block, Thunder Wave, Rock Slide, Sandstorm, Rest, Zap Cannon, Lock On
Evolution: None
Height: 1m/3'3"
Weight: 97kg/214lb

61 SKITTY

Category: Kitten
Type: Normal
Attacks: Growl, Tackle, Tail Whip, Sing, Doubleslap, Attract, Assist, Charm, Faint Attack, Covet, Heal Bell, Double Edge
Evolution: >Delcatty
Height: 0.6m/2'0"
Weight: 11kg/24lb

66 TENTACOOL

Category: Jellyfish
Type: Water/Poison
Attacks: Poison Sting, Supersonic, Constrict, Acid, Bubblebeam, Wrap, Barrier, Screech, Hydro Pump
Evolution: >Tentacruel
Height: 0.9m/2'11"
Weight: 45.5kg/100lb

62 DELCATTY

Category: Prim
Type: Normal
Attacks: Growl, Sing, Attract, Doubleslap
Evolution: None
Height: 1.1m/3'7"
Weight: 32.6kg/72lb

67 TENTACRUEL

Category: Jellyfish
Type: Water/Poison
Attacks: Poison Sting, Supersonic, Constrict, Acid, Bubblebeam, Wrap, Barrier, Screech, Hydro Pump
Evolution: None
Height: 1.6m/5'3"
Weight: 55kg/121lb

63 ZUBAT

Category: Bat
Type: Poison/Flying
Attacks: Leech Life, Supersonic, Astonish, Bite, Wing Attack, Confuse Ray, Air Cutter, Mean Look, Poison Fang, Haze
Evolution: >Golbat >Crobat
Height: 0.8m/2'7"
Weight: 7.5kg/17lb

68 SABLEYE

Category: Darkness
Type: Dark/Ghost
Attacks: Leer, Scratch, Foresight, Night Shade, Astonish, Fury Swipes, Fake Out, Detect, Faint Attack, Knock Off, Confuse Ray, Shadow Ball, Mean Look
Evolution: None
Height: 0.5m/1'8"
Weight: 11kg/24lb.

64 GOLBAT

Category: Bat
Type: Poison/Flying
Attacks: Screech, Leech Life, Supersonic, Astonish, Bite, Wing Attack, Confuse Ray, Air Cutter, Mean Look, Poison Fang, Haze
Evolution: >Crobat
Height: 1.6m/5'3"
Weight: 55kg/121lb

69 MAWILE

Category: Deceiver
Type: Steel
Attacks: Astonish, Fake Tears, Bite, Sweet Scent, Vicegrip, Faint Attack, Baton Pass, Crunch, Iron Defence, Stockpile, Swallow, Spit Up
Evolution: None
Height: 0.6m/2'0"
Weight: 11.5kg/25lb

65 CROBAT

Category: Bat
Type: Poison/Flying
Attacks: Screech, Leech Life, Supersonic, Astonish, Bite, Wing Attack, Confuse Ray, Air Cutter, Mean Look, Poison Fang, Haze
Evolution: None
Height: 1.8m/5'11"
Weight: 75kg/165lb

70 ARON

Category: Iron Armour
Type: Steel/Rock
Attacks: Tackle, Harden, Mud Slap, Headbutt, Metal Claw, Iron Defence, Roar, Take Down, Iron Tail, Protect, Metal Sound, Double Edge
Evolution: >Lairon >Aggron
Height: 0.4m/1'4"
Weight: 60kg/132lb

71 LAIRON

Category: Iron Armour
Type: Steel/Rock
Attacks: Tackle, Harden, Mud Slap, Headbutt, Metal Claw, Iron Defence, Roar, Take Down, Iron Tail, Protect, Metal Sound, Double Edge
Evolution: >Aggron
Height: 0.9m/2'11"
Weight: 120kg/265lb

76 MEDITITE

Category: Meditate
Type: Fighting/Psychic
Attacks: Bide, Meditate, Confusion, Detect, Hidden Power, Mind Reader, Calm Mind, Hi Jump Kick, Psych Up, Reversal, Recover
Evolution: >Medicham
Height: 0.6m/2'0"
Weight: 11.2kg/25lb

72 AGGRON

Category: Iron Armour
Type: Steel/Rock
Attacks: Tackle, Harden, Mud Slap, Headbutt, Metal Claw, Iron Defence, Roar, Take Down, Iron Tail, Protect, Metal Sound, Double Edge
Evolution: None
Height: 2.1m/6'11"
Weight: 360kg/794lb

77 MEDICHAM

Category: Meditate
Type: Fighting/Psychic
Attacks: Fire Punch, Thunderpunch, Ice Punch, Bide, Meditate, Confusion, Detect, Hidden Power, Mind Reader, Calm Mind, Hi Jump Kick, Psych Up, Reversal, Recover
Evolution: >None
Height: 1.3m/4'3"
Weight: 31.5kg/69lb

73 MACHOP

Category: Superpower
Type: Fighting
Attacks: Low Kick, Leer, Focus Energy, Karate Chop, Seismic Toss, Foresight, Revenge, Vital Throw, Submission, Cross Chop, Scary Face, Dynamicpunch
Evolution: >Machoke >Machamp
Height: 0.8m/2'7"
Weight: 19.5kg/43lb

78 ELECTRIKE

Category: Lightning
Type: Electric
Attacks: Tackle, Thunder Wave, Leer, Howl, Quick Attack, Spark, Odour Sleuth, Roar, Bite, Thunder, Charge
Evolution: >Manectric
Height: 0.6m/2'0"
Weight: 15.2kg/34lb

74 MACHOKE

Category: Superpower
Type: Fighting
Attacks: Low Kick, Leer, Focus Energy, Karate Chop, Seismic Toss, Foresight, Revenge, Vital Throw, Submission, Cross Chop, Scary Face, Dynamicpunch
Evolution: >Machamp
Height: 1.5m/4'11"
Weight: 70.5kg/155lb

79 MANECTRIC

Category: Discharge
Type: Electric
Attacks: Tackle, Thunder Wave, Leer, Howl, Quick Attack, Spark, Odour Sleuth, Roar, Bite, Thunder, Charge
Evolution: None
Height: 1.5m/4'11"
Weight: 40.2kg/89lb

75 MACHAMP

Category: Superpower
Type: Fighting
Attacks: Low Kick, Leer, Focus Energy, Karate Chop, Seismic Toss, Foresight, Revenge, Vital Throw, Submission, Cross Chop, Scary Face, Dynamicpunch
Evolution: None
Height: 1.6m/5'3"
Weight: 130kg/287lb

80 PLUSLE

Category: Cheering
Type: Electric
Attacks: Growl, Thunder Wave, Quick Attack, Helping Hand, Spark, Encore, Fake Tears, Charge, Thunder, Baton Pass, Agility
Evolution: None
Height: 0.4m/1'4"
Weight: 4.2kg/9lb

POKÉMON ARTIST

Colour in this cool picture of Ash and his new Pokémon friends. Copy the colours in the picture opposite.

THERE'S NO PLACE LIKE HOENN

On the way to Oldale Town, May tried to battle her Torchic against an Azurill. But she forgot all Torchic's attacks, and it got hurt!

When they reached Oldale Town they went straight to the Pokémon Centre. The nurse took care of Torchic, while Ash and May registered for the Hoenn League. "I can't wait to get my first badge!" Ash grinned.

Later they met Professor Aldon, who was researching the ancient ruins in Oldale Town.

"The stone chamber in the ruins is supposed to be a portal to the ancient Pokémon world," the professor told them. "But to enter you need four keys – and nobody knows where they are!"

"What are ancient Pokémon?" Ash asked.

"They're Pokémon that have been living since ancient times, without changing at all!" explained the professor.

"How cool!" said Ash.

Suddenly, the doors burst open and a team of masked figures rushed in!

"Professor," said one of them, "You're coming to the Oldale ruins!"

Professor Aldon struggled but they dragged him away, locking May, Ash and Nurse Joy in the room!
"Hey! Let us outta here!" yelled Ash.
Just then, Pikachu noticed an airshaft in the corner of the room.

They crawled down the shaft and were soon back in the main entrance hall.
"Who were those people?" May wondered.
"I dunno," said Ash, "but right now we've gotta help Professor Aldon!"

May and Ash arrived at the ruins just in time to see a huge helicopter taking off. They found Professor Aldon outside the stone chamber! "Are you all right?" cried May.

"I'm fine," said the professor. "Those people had the keys to the chamber, but as you can see, it's empty! It told them nothing!"

Just then the rays of the rising sun shone onto the four keys in the door. The chamber was filled with magical light! Then the door moved aside, revealing a flight of steps!

"Amazing!" gasped the professor. "They left before the sun came up, so they didn't see the real mysteries of the chamber!"

Professor Aldon led them down the steps to a vast underground lake. They saw a strange-looking Pokémon in the water.

"The ancient Pokémon Relicanth!" cried Professor Aldon. "I can't wait to begin my research on this cavern!"

"This place is awesome, professor!" grinned Ash.
"Did those people say who they were?" asked May.
"No," replied the professor. "But to be honest, I'm more interested in uncovering the mysteries of ancient Pokémon!"
"And right now it's time for us to head for Petalburg City," Ash added.
"I've got my first badge to win!"

The leader of the Petalburg gym was May's father, Norman! May showed her parents her first Pokémon.

"Torchic's a great Pokémon to start out with," said her father.

"It's as cute as a button, May!" her mother smiled. May's little brother, Max, loved Pokémon too.

"You were in the Johto League Silver Conference!" he said eagerly. "You lost in the second round!"

"It was the championship tournament!" growled Ash.

"Dad, Ash would like to have a gym battle with you," said May.

"Of course!" agreed Norman. It won't be an official gym battle though. The rules say it's a three on three elimination, and you only have one!"

"That's okay," smiled Ash, "I still really appreciate it – thank you!"

Norman and Ash faced each other across the gym.
"Vigoroth, I choose you!" cried Norman.
Vigoroth the wild monkey appeared – going berserk!

"Pika!" Pikachu gasped.
"We'll just have to do the best we can,"
said Ash. "Pikachu – GO!"

Pikachu fought bravely – Scratch Attack! Quick Attack! Thunderbolt! But
Vigoroth was just too strong – and in the end Ash and Pikachu were beaten.
"That Vigoroth is really powerful!" said Ash, shaking hands with Norman after
the battle.

Norman had a favour to ask.

"Ash, would it be okay if Max travelled with you and May? He knows a lot about Pokémon, and he might be a big help to you!"

"That's fine," smiled Ash.

"This is gonna be awesome!" Max cheered. "Where are we heading, Ash?"

"I suggest that you travel to the nearest gym, and that's in Rustboro City," said Norman.

Norman gave Max a Pokémon Navigator as a leaving present.

"I've always wanted one of these!" gasped Max. "Thanks, Dad!"

"Now you'll always know exactly where you are," Norman smiled.

As they walked through Petalburg Woods towards Rustboro City, Max kept a lookout for Pokémon through his binoculars.

"Any chance we'll be stopping to eat soon?" complained May.

"But I haven't even seen one Pokémon yet!" wailed Max.

Then Ash realised that they had forgotten the lunch! There wasn't even any Pokémon energy for Pikachu and Torchic!

"It's too bad that Brock didn't come along with us," sighed Ash.

"Who?" asked Max and May.

"Brock's a friend I was travelling with before," Ash told them. "He knows lots about Pokémon... but he really knows how to cook, too!"

Then Max remembered something.
"My emergency stash!" he grinned, pulling a chocolate cookie out of his bag.
But before he could share it out, a flying Pokémon swooped down and stole it!
"Our chocolate!" wailed May.

"Hey, look guys!" Ash
exclaimed. "These trees are
full of fruit!"
But when Pikachu knocked
some of the fruit down
with its Thunderbolt,
the whole flock of
Taillow attacked!

"Taillow never back down!" yelled Ash. "They're really fierce!"
Pikachu attacked the Taillow bravely, but his lightning attacks only slowed them down.
"They're closing in on us!" screamed May.
"Nothing seems to work!" yelled Ash.
"Forretress, EXPLOSION!" cried a voice from behind them. There was a burst of powerful energy as a Forretress Pokémon fought off the Taillow, then returned to its trainer...

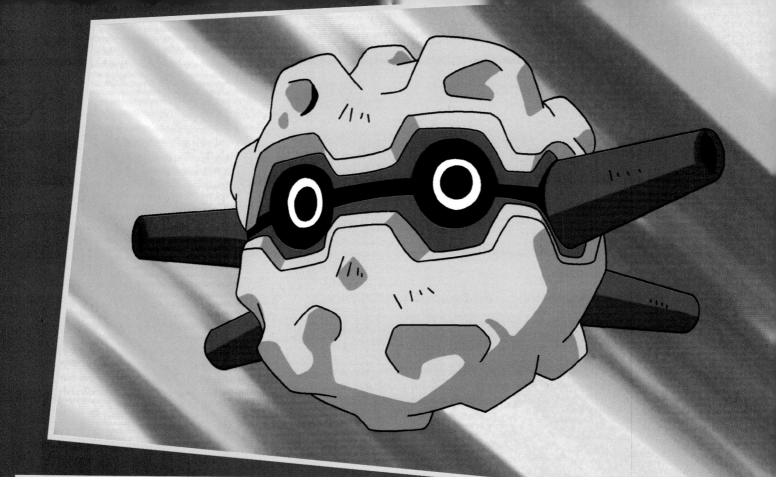

"Brock!" cried Ash in delight. "What are you doing here? I thought you were going home!"

"I decided to come back out and see if I could find you," grinned Brock.

"Does that mean we're gonna travel together again?"

"Yes – if you don't mind?"

"Best news I've had all day," grinned Ash.

As Ash introduced Brock to Max and May, a single Taillow flew down and landed opposite Pikachu.

"It looks angry," said Brock. "A strong opponent always makes Taillow want to battle."

"We accept!" said Ash. "Let's go, Pikachu! Quick Attack!"

Pikachu launched its first attack, but Taillow dodged it easily.

"First attacks are almost never off target!" gasped Max. "How could it have dodged that?"

Pikachu battled hard, but Taillow wouldn't give up!

"Wow, that Taillow's awesome!" exclaimed Ash. "It just won't back down!"

Taillow was hurt, but kept going!

"You should put an end to this battle before you do it any more damage," said Brock. You'll have to catch it!"

Ash threw a Poké Ball and caught the Taillow.

"My very first Pokémon here in the Hoenn Region!" he grinned.

Soon Brock had got to work and made everyone a delicious stew.
"Ash wasn't kidding – you're an awesome cook, Brock," said May happily.
"Time for us to get moving," said Ash. "Let's head out to Rustboro City!"

WHATS YOUR TEAM?

Check out your style with this quiz, and find out which team you belong with. Better hope it's not Team Rocket!

1. In Petalburg Forest you meet a trainer with an amazing Mudkip Pokémon. Do you…
   a) Challenge her to a battle?
   b) Launch a surprise attack and steal her Pokémon?
   c) Dig a pitfall trap and hope she falls into it?

2. In the Oldale Town ruins you spot a Pokémon you've never seen before. Do you…
   a) Check it out on your Pokédex?
   b) Challenge it to a battle?
   c) Run away!

3. You are out in the mountains with Professor Birch when a Poochyena attacks him. Do you…
   a) Grab a Poké Ball and try to help?
   b) Take the opportunity to 'borrow' Professor Birch's Poké Balls?
   c) Remember an urgent appointment in town?

4. Your opponent has a much stronger Pokémon than you. Do you…
   a) Battle him anyway and hope you can beat him with superior strategy?
   b) Blast him with your strongest attack while he isn't looking, then make a quick getaway?
   c) Remember another urgent appointment in town?

5. You've run out of Pokémon energy and there isn't another Pokémon Centre for miles! Do you…
a) Keep your eyes out for another Pokémon trainer and ask to buy some of their energy?
b) Nothing. It will do the Pokémon good to learn how to survive without energy!
c) Panic?

6. An evil genius has bred a super-Pokémon to try and take over the world. Do you…
a) Stand and fight? Everyone has to do their best to stop this madman!
b) Offer to join him and strengthen his chances with your Pokémon?
c) Hide and hope he goes away?

7. The Petalburg gym is in danger! There is a rockslide in the mountains above it, and the gym is in the way! Do you…
a) Help everyone escape, risking your own life?
b) Take the chance to sneak in and steal the gym's secrets?
c) Forget about the others – save yourself?

8. You are attacked by a flock of Taillow. Do you…
a) Try to figure out why they are attacking you – have you accidentally done something to upset them?
b) Blast them with Hyper Beam – they shouldn't get in your way!
c) Run and hide?

HOW YOU SCORED?

Mostly A: Hey – you and Ash would make a great team! You're a Master Trainer in the making!

Mostly B: You're certainly brave, but you don't care who gets in your way! You should join mysterious Team Magma!

Mostly C: Oh dear. You'd better go and join Team Rocket – if you're brave enough!

THE RACE IS ON

Join the race to Rustboro City for your first gym battle in the Hoenn Region! The winner is the first person to reach the Rustboro City gym and challenge the gym leader.

	Go back 1 space	Go forward 3 spaces

Go forward 2 spaces		Go back 1 space	Miss a turn

		Go forward 3 spaces	

game for 2 or more players.
ou will need: a marker for each player and 2 dice.
ow to play:
Flip a coin to decide who goes first.
Throw the dice and move your marker that number of squares along the Pokémon trail.
Check out the instructions on the square where you land and do what they say!
The first trainer to reach Rustboro City gym is the winner!

Have another turn

Go forward 2 spaces

Go back to start

ve another turn

Go back 3 spaces

Miss a turn

81 MINUN

Category: Cheering
Type: Electric
Attacks: Growl, Thunder Wave, Quick Attack, Helping Hand, Spark, Encore, Charm, Charge, Thunder, Baton Pass, Agility
Evolution: None
Height: 0.4m/1'4"
Weight: 4.2kg/9lb

86 VOLBEAT

Category: Firefly
Type: Bug
Attacks: Tackle, Confuse Ray, Double Team, Moonlight, Quick Attack, Tail Glow, Signal Beam, Protect, Helping Hand, Double Edge
Evolution: None
Height: 0.7m/2'4"
Weight: 17.7kg/39lb

82 MAGNEMITE

Category: Magnet
Type: Electric/Steel
Attacks: Metal Sound, Tackle, Thundershock, Supersonic, Sonicboom, Thunder Wave, Spark, Lock On, Swift, Screech, Zap Cannon
Evolution: >Magneton
Height: 0.3m/1'0"
Weight: 6kg/13lb

87 ILLUMISE

Category: Firefly
Type: Bug
Attacks: Tackle, Sweet Scent, Charm, Moonlight, Quick Attack, Wish, Encore, Flatter, Helping Hand, Covet
Evolution: None
Height: 0.6m/2'0"
Weight: 17.7kg/39lb

83 MAGNETON

Category: Magnet
Type: Electric/Steel
Attacks: Metal Sound, Tackle, Thundershock, Supersonic, Sonicboom, Thunder Wave, Spark, Lock On, Tri Attack, Screech, Zap Cannon
Evolution: None
Height: 1m/3'3"
Weight: 60kg/132lb

88 ODDISH

Category: Weed
Type: Grass/Poison
Attacks: Absorb, Sweet Scent, Poisonpowder, Stun Spore, Sleep Powder, Acid, Moonlight, Petal Dance
Evolution: > Gloom >Vileplume >Bellossom
Height: 0.5m/1'8"
Weight: 5.4kg/12lb

84 VOLTORB

Category: Ball
Type: Electric
Attacks: Charge, Tackle, Screech, Sonicboom, Spark, Selfdestruct, Rollout, Light Screen, Swift, Explosion, Mirror Coat
Evolution: >Electrode
Height: 0.5m/1'8"
Weight: 10.4kg/23lb

89 GLOOM

Category: Weed
Type: Grass/Poison
Attacks: Absorb, Sweet Scent, Poisonpowder, Stun Spore, Sleep Powder, Acid, Moonlight, Petal Dance
Evolution: >Vileplume >Bellossom
Height: 0.8m/2'7"
Weight: 8.6kg/19lb

85 ELECTRODE

Category: Ball
Type: Electric
Attacks: Charge, Tackle, Screech, Sonicboom, Spark, Selfdestruct, Rollout, Light Screen, Swift, Explosion, Mirror Coat
Evolution: None
Height: 1.2m/3'11"
Weight: 66.6kg/147lb

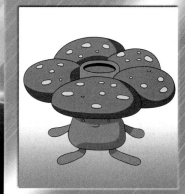

90 VILEPLUME

Category: Flower
Type: Grass/Poison
Attacks: Absorb, Aromatherapy, Stun Spore, Mega Drain, Petal Dance
Evolution: >Bellossom
Height: 1.2m/3'11"
Weight: 18.6kg/41lb

91 BELLOSSOM

Category: Flower
Type: Grass
Attacks: Absorb, Sweet Scent, Stun Spore, Magical Leaf, Petal Dance, Solarbeam
Evolution: None
Height: 0.4m/1'4"
Weight: 5.8kg/13lb

92 DODUO

Category: Twin Bird
Type: Normal/Flying
Attacks: Peck, Growl, Pursuit, Fury Attack, Tri Attack, Rage, Uproar, Drill Peck, Agility
Evolution: >Dodrio
Height: 1.4m/4'7"
Weight: 39.2kg/86lb

93 DODRIO

Category: Triple Bird
Type: Normal/Flying
Attacks: Peck, Growl, Pursuit, Fury Attack, Tri Attack, Rage, Uproar, Drill Peck, Agility
Evolution: None
Height: 1.8m/5'11"
Weight: 85.2kg/188lb

94 ROSELIA

Category: Thorn
Type: Grass/Poison
Attacks: Absorb, Growth, Poison Sting, Stun Spore, Mega Drain, Leech Seed, Magical Leaf, Grasswhistle, Giga Drain, Sweet Scent, Ingrain, Toxic, Petal Dance, Aromatherapy, Synthesis
Evolution: None
Height: 0.3m/1'0"
Weight: 2kg/4lb

95 GULPIN

Category: Stomach
Type: Poison
Attacks: Pound, Yawn, Poison Gas, Sludge, Amnesia, Encore, Toxic, Stockpile, Spit Up, Swallow, Sludge Bomb
Evolution: >Swalot
Height: 0.4m/1'4"
Weight: 10.3kg/23lb

96 SWALOT

Category: Poison Bag
Type: Poison
Attacks: Pound, Yawn, Poison Gas, Sludge, Amnesia, Encore, Body Slam, Toxic, Stockpile, Spit Up, Swallow, Sludge Bomb
Evolution: None
Height: 1.7m/5'7"
Weight: 80kg/176lb

97 CARVANHA

Category: Savage
Type: Water/Dark
Attacks: Leer, Bite, Rage, Focus Energy, Scary Face, Crunch, Screech, Take Down, Swagger, Agility
Evolution: >Sharpedo
Height: 0.8m/2'7"
Weight: 20.8kg/46lb

98 SHARPEDO

Category: Brutal
Type: Water/Dark
Attacks: Leer, Bite, Rage, Focus Energy, Scary Face, Crunch, Screech, Slash, Taunt, Swagger, Skull Bash, Agility
Evolution: None
Height: 1.8m/5'11"
Weight: 88.8kg/196lb

99 WAILMER

Category: Ball Whale
Type: Water
Attacks: Splash, Growl, Water Gun, Rollout, Whirlpool, Astonish, Water Pulse, Mist, Rest, Water Spout, Amnesia, Hydro Pump
Evolution: >Wailord
Height: 2m/6'7"
Weight: 130kg/287lb

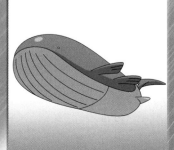

100 WAILORD

Category: Float Whale
Type: Water
Attacks: Splash, Growl, Water Gun, Rollout, Whirlpool, Astonish, Water Pulse, Mist, Rest, Water Spout, Amnesia, Hydro Pump
Evolution: None
Height: 14.5m/47'7"
Weight: 398kg/878lb

101 NUMEL

Category: Numb
Type: Fire/Ground
Attacks: Growl, Tackle, Ember, Magnitude, Focus Energy, Take Down, Amnesia, Earthquake, Flamethrower, Double Edge
Evolution: >Camerupt
Height: 0.7m/2'4"
Weight: 24kg/53lb

106 GRIMER

Category: Sludge
Type: Poison
Attacks: Poison Gas, Pound, Harden, Disable, Sludge, Minimise, Screech, Acid Armour, Sludge Bomb, Memento
Evolution: >Muk
Height: 0.9m/2'11"
Weight: 30kg/66lb

102 CAMERUPT

Category: Eruption
Type: Fire/Ground
Attacks: Growl, Tackle, Ember, Magnitude, Focus Energy, Take Down, Amnesia, Rock Slide, Earthquake, Eruption, Fissure
Evolution: None
Height: 1.9m/6'3"
Weight: 220kg/485lb

107 MUK

Category: Sludge
Type: Poison
Attacks: Poison Gas, Pound, Harden, Disable, Sludge, Minimise, Screech, Acid Armour, Sludge Bomb, Memento
Evolution: None
Height: 1.2m/3'11"
Weight: 30kg/66lb

103 SLUGMA

Category: Lava
Type: Fire
Attacks: Yawn, Smog, Ember, Rock Throw, Harden, Amnesia, Flamethrower, Rock Slide, Body Slam
Evolution: >Magcargo
Height: 0.7m/2'4"
Weight: 35kg/77lb

108 KOFFING

Category: Poison Gas
Type: Poison
Attacks: Poison Gas, Tackle, Smog, Selfdestruct, Sludge, Smokescreen, Haze, Explosion, Destiny Bond, Memento
Evolution: >Weezing
Height: 0.6m/2'0"
Weight: 1kg/2lb

104 MAGCARGO

Category: Lava
Type: Fire/Rock
Attacks: Yawn, Smog, Ember, Rock Throw, Harden, Amnesia, Flamethrower, Rock Slide, Body Slam
Evolution: None
Height: 0.8m/2'7"
Weight: 55kg/121lb

109 WEEZING

Category: Poison Gas
Type: Poison
Attacks: Poison Gas, Tackle, Sludge, Smog, Selfdestruct, Smokescreen, Haze, Explosion, Destiny Bond, Memento
Evolution: None
Height: 1.2m/3'11"
Weight: 9.5kg/21lb

105 TORKOAL

Category: Coal
Type: Fire
Attacks: Ember, Smog, Curse, Smokescreen, Fire Spin, Body Slam, Protect, Flamethrower, Iron Defence, Amnesia, Flail, Heat Wave
Evolution: None
Height: 0.5m/1'8"
Weight: 80.4kg/177lb

110 SPOINK

Category: Bounce
Type: Psychic
Attacks: Splash, Psywave, Odour Sleuth, Psybeam, Psych Up, Confuse Ray, Magic Coat, Psychic, Rest, Snore, Bounce
Evolution: >Grumpig
Height: 0.7m/2'4"
Weight: 30.6kg/67lb

111 GRUMPIG

Category: Manipulate
Type: Psychic
Attacks: Splash, Psywave, Odour Sleuth, Psybeam, Psych Up, Confuse Ray, Magic Coat, Psychic, Rest, Snore, Bounce
Evolution: None
Height: 0.9m/2'11"
Weight: 71.5kg/158lb

112 SANDSHREW

Category: Mouse
Type: Ground
Attacks: Scratch, Defence Curl, Sand Attack, Poison Sting, Slash, Swift, Fury Swipes, Sand Tomb, Sandstorm
Evolution: >Sandslash
Height: 0.6m/2'0"
Weight: 12kg/26lb

113 SANDSLASH

Category: Mouse
Type: Ground
Attacks: Scratch, Defence Curl, Sand Attack, Poison Sting, Slash, Swift, Fury Swipes, Sand Tomb, Sandstorm
Evolution: None
Height: 1m/3'3"
Weight: 29.5kg/65lb

114 SPINDA

Category: Spot Panda
Type: Normal
Attacks: Tackle, Uproar, Faint Attack, Psybeam, Hypnosis, Dizzy Punch, Teeter Dance, Psych Up, Double Edge, Flail, Thrash
Evolution: None
Height: 1.1m/3'7"
Weight: 5kg/11lb

115 SKARMORY

Category: Armor Bird
Type: Steel/Flying
Attacks: Leer, Peck, Sand Attack, Swift, Agility, Fury Attack, Air Cutter, Steel Wing, Spikes, Metal Sound
Evolution: None
Height: 1.7m/5'7"
Weight: 50.5kg/111lb

116 TRAPINCH

Category: Ant Pit
Type: Ground
Attacks: Bite, Sand Attack, Faint Attack, Sand Tomb, Crunch, Dig, Sandstorm, Hyper Beam
Evolution: >Vibrava >Flygon
Height: 0.7m/2'4"
Weight: 15kg/33lb

117 VIBRAVA

Category: Vibration
Type: Ground/Dragon
Attacks: Bite, Sand Attack, Faint Attack, Sand Tomb, Crunch, Dragonbreath, Screech, Sandstorm, Hyper Beam
Evolution: >Flygon
Height: 1.1m/3'7"
Weight: 15.3kg/34lb

118 FLYGON

Category: Mystic
Type: Ground/Dragon
Attacks: Bite, Sand Attack, Faint Attack, Sand Tomb, Crunch, Dragonbreath, Screech, Sandstorm, Hyper Beam
Evolution: None
Height: 2m/6'7"
Weight: 82kg/181lb

119 CACNEA

Category: Cactus
Type: Grass
Attacks: Poison Sting, Leer, Absorb, Growth, Leech Seed, Sand Attack, Pin Missile, Ingrain, Faint Attack, Spikes, Needle Arm, Cotton Spore, Sandstorm
Evolution: >Cacturne
Height: 0.4m/1'4"
Weight: 51.3kg/113lb

120 CACTURNE

Category: Scarecrow
Type: Grass/Dark
Attacks: Poison Sting, Leer, Absorb, Growth, Leech Seed, Sand Attack, Pin Missile, Ingrain, Faint Attack, Spikes, Needle Arm, Cotton Spore, Sandstorm
Evolution: None
Height: 1.3m/4'3"
Weight: 77.4kg/171lb

IN THE KNICKER OF TIME

On the way to Rustboro City, Ash stopped to battle a trainer they met in the forest. Ash won and he and his opponent shook hands.

"Thanks for an incredible battle," said the boy.

"I should be thanking you!" grinned Ash.

May was impressed. "Two trainers ending their battle with a warm handshake," she said. "Now that's true sportsmanship!"

"That's what Pokémon battling is really all about," nodded Brock. "Friendship!"

"That's for sure," agreed Ash. "If you're not making friends, what's the point?"

As they set off again, something darted out on the path in front of them.
"A Zigzagoon!" Max said. "But it's enormous!"
"There are more of them," pointed May. "But the others are much smaller."
Suddenly the big Zigzagoon rose up on its back legs and seemed to throw off its coat! It was a boy!
"It's disguised itself as a human!" May shrieked.
"It is a human!" said Max.

The boy saw them and stared at Max and May's shorts in amazement.
"Hey – cool! You guys are wearing knickers too! You're the same as me!"
"Who are you?" exclaimed Ash.

"I have many names!" the boy grinned. Before their amazed eyes he turned into three different Pokémon!

"At times I am a Zigzagoon wandering the forest! Sometimes I am a dancing Bellossom or a Tentacruel! But my true identity is... Nicholai the Knicker Bocker!"

"What's a Knicker Bocker?" asked Ash.

"That's the name for naturalist trainers! Obviously you're Knicker Bockers too! So what are your names?"

"Listen," said May when they had introduced themselves, "These are shorts – we're not Knicker Bockers!"

"Why were you dressed in that Zigzagoon suit?" asked Brock.

"To learn the Pokémon's inner feelings – when I know the way they're thinking, it's easy to capture them! I wanna challenge the Petalburg gym leader, but first I'm gonna catch a Zigzagoon."

"You'll be battling our Dad!" said Max.

"Wow!" said Nicholai. "It would be great practice to battle the children of a gym leader!"

"Show him what you can do, May!" cheered Max.

"Uh, I don't think I can–" May stammered.

"Are you afraid?" grinned Nicholai.

"Me, afraid?" blazed May. "Okay – I accept!"

"Mudkip, let's go!" cried Nicholai, transforming into a Mudkip.

"Choose your Pokémon, May!" called Brock.

"Oh, right!" said May nervously. "Torchic, I choose you!"

"Her first opponent would have to have a water Pokémon!" groaned Max.

"She can use good strategy to make up for it!" said Ash.

"This is May we're talking about," Max sighed.

"Tell Torchic what attack to use!" called Ash.

"Oh! Uh, Torchic – Ember!" shouted May. But Mudkip's Water Gun extinguished Torchic's attack!

"Torchic, Peck Attack!" cried May.

"Don't attack it from straight on!" called Max. But it was too late! Torchic got the full blast of Mudkip's Water Gun!

"Torchic is unable to battle. Mudkip's the winner!" announced Brock.

"Unreal!" gloated Nicholai. "Who knew a gym leader's daughter would be so bad? Getting a badge at the Petalburg gym'll be a piece of cake!"

"Take that back!" yelled Max.

"But first I have to catch a Zigzagoon," continued Nicholai. "Goodbye, my fellow Knicker Bockers!"

Hidden nearby, Team Rocket had watched the battle eagerly.
"That Mudkip's amazing!" said James. "We should catch it!"
"The boss'd promote us for sure!" Meowth agreed.
"Operation Mudkip Capture!" said Jessie.

"My very first battle and it ends in defeat!" May groaned. "I can't wait until Dad beats that weirdo, right Max?"
But there was no reply. Max had disappeared!

"No one makes fun of my Dad and gets away with it," Max growled. He hurried back along the path and soon saw Nicholai, carrying some fruit.

"Zigzagoon love that fruit," thought Max. He picked an armful of fruit and went looking for Zigzagoon.

"All this fruit ought to attract every Zigzagoon in the forest!" he thought. "That Knicker Bocker won't catch a single one!"

Ash, May and Brock found Max surrounded by Zigzagoon!
"I didn't realise there were so many!" cried Max. "Help!"
Brock tried to share the fruit among the Zigzagoon, but they were angry and started to attack!
Suddenly Nicholai appeared in his Zigzagoon suit. He talked to the Pokémon, and after a moment they all followed him! He led them to some fruit trees.
"Mudkip – Water Gun!" said Nicholai. Mudkip's attack knocked lots of fruit from the trees, and all the Zigzagoon settled down happily to eat!

"Thanks Nicholai!" grinned Ash. "You really helped us out!"

"Us Knicker Bockers have to stick together!" laughed Nicholai.

"I owe you an apology" said Max.

"Forget it – I shouldn't have made fun of your dad. Which reminds me – I still need to catch a Zigzagoon!" He pointed at a Zigzagoon nearby. "Hey – how would you like to battle us?"

The Zigzagoon accepted the challenge.

"Mudkip – Water Gun!" began Nicholai.

The Zigzagoon charged straight at Mudkip! It was going to be a tough battle!

"That Mudkip and Zigzagoon are amazing!" said May.

At last the Zigzagoon weakened and Nicholai threw a Poké Ball. It worked!

"Yes!" cheered Nicholai. "I caught a Zigzagoon!"

Suddenly a metal pincer descended from the sky and grabbed Mudkip! It was Team Rocket!

"Your Mudkip!" gasped Ash.

"I'm sorry, whose Mudkip did you say it was?" Jessie smirked.

"Who do you think you are?" roared Nicholai. "Give me back my Mudkip!"

"Pikachu, Thunderbolt!" yelled Ash. But a reflective shield shot out of the balloon and the Thunderbolt attack rebounded!

"Pokémon – change!" shouted Nicholai, transforming into Aipon and dashing after the balloon. "Don't worry, Mudkip – I'm coming!"

As Nicholai raced after the balloon, the Zigzagoon started to dig.
"What are they doing?" wondered May.
Nicholai transformed into a Gligar and leaped off a cliff above the
balloon. He glided past and grabbed the cage from James!

"You're safe now, Mudkip!" said Nicholai, landing next to Ash.
"Taillow!" shouted Ash. "Peck Attack!"
Taillow darted up and pecked a hole in the balloon. It plummeted to the ground and Team Rocket landed in a deep hole!
"That's what the Zigzagoon were digging!" laughed Max.

Team Rocket clambered furiously out of the hole.
"You're not going anywhere!" said Ash.
"Just watch us!" fumed Jessie. "Arbok – Poison Sting!"
"Weezing – you too!" yelled James. "Sludge Attack!"
But Ash was ready for them.
"Pikachu – Quick Attack!" he said. Arbok and Weezing fell back.

"Now, Thunder Attack – GO!" shouted Ash.
Team Rocket blasted off into the distance!"That was some pretty slick battling!" said Nicholai.
"Thanks – I just wish it went that well when I battled the leader of the Petalburg gym!" grinned Ash.
"Maybe it won't be so easy to get that badge after all..."
"Yeah," said Max, "My sister's pretty lame, but my Dad's tough!"
"Would you battle with me, Ash?" asked Nicholai.
"I was hoping you'd ask!" said Ash.

As Nicholai and Ash faced each other with Zigzagoon and Taillow, Max grinned.
"How cool! Since they're both fighting with new Pokémon, it's almost like they're having a battle for the very first time!"
"I guess everyone still has a lot to learn!" smiled May.

81

121 SWABLU

Category: Cotton Bird
Type: Normal/Flying
Attacks: Peck, Growl, Astonish, Sing, Fury Attack, Safeguard, Mist, Take Down, Mirror Move, Refresh, Perish Song
Evolution: >Altaria
Height: 0.4m/1'4"
Weight: 1.2kg/3lb

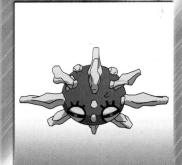

126 SOLROCK

Category: Meteorite
Type: Rock/Psychic
Attacks: Tackle, Harden, Confusion, Rock Throw, Fire Spin, Psywave, Cosmic Power, Rock Slide, Solarbeam, Explosion
Evolution: None
Height: 1.2m/3'11"
Weight: 154kg/340lb

122 ALTARIA

Category: Humming
Type: Dragon/Flying
Attacks: Peck, Growl, Astonish, Sing, Fury Attack, Safeguard, Mist, Take Down, Dragonbreath, Dragon Dance, Refresh, Perish Song, Sky Attack
Evolution: None
Height: 1.1m/3'7"
Weight: 20.6kg/45lb

127 BARBOACH

Category: Whiskers
Type: Water/Ground
Attacks: Mud Slap, Mud Sport, Water Sport, Water Gun, Magnitude, Amnesia, Rest, Snore, Earthquake, Future Sight, Fissure
Evolution: >Whiscash
Height: 0.4m/1'4"
Weight: 1.9kg/4lb

123 ZANGOOSE

Category: Cat Ferret
Type: Normal
Attacks: Scratch, Leer, Quick Attack, Swords Dance, Fury Cutter, Slash, Pursuit, Crush Claw, Taunt, Detect, False Swipe
Evolution: None
Height: 1.3m/4'3"
Weight: 40.3kg/89lb

128 WHISCASH

Category: Whiskers
Type: Water/Ground
Attacks: Tickle, Mud Slap, Mud Sport, Water Sport, Water Gun, Magnitude, Amnesia, Rest, Snore, Earthquake, Future Sight, Fissure
Evolution: None
Height: 0.9m/2'11"
Weight: 23.6kg/52lb

124 SEVIPER

Category: Fang Snake
Type: Poison
Attacks: Wrap, Lick, Bite, Poison Tail, Screech, Glare, Crunch, Poison Fang, Swagger, Haze
Evolution: None
Height: 2.7m/8'10"
Weight: 52.5kg/116kg

129 CORPHISH

Category: Ruffian
Type: Water
Attacks: Bubble, Harden, Vicegrip, Leer, Bubblebeam, Protect, Knock Off, Taunt, Crabhammer, Swords Dance, Guillotine
Evolution: >Crawdaunt
Height: 0.6m/2'0"
Weight: 11.5kg/25lb

125 LUNATONE

Category: Meteorite
Type: Rock/Psychic
Attacks: Tackle, Harden, Confusion, Rock Throw, Hypnosis, Psywave, Cosmic Power, Psychic, Future Sight, Explosion
Evolution: None
Height: 1m/3'3"
Weight: 168kg/370lb

130 CRAWDAUNT

Category: Rogue
Type: Water/Dark
Attacks: Bubble, Harden, Vicegrip, Leer, Bubblebeam, Protect, Knock Off, Taunt, Crabhammer, Swords Dance, Guillotine
Evolution: None
Height: 1.1m/3'7"
Weight: 32.8kg/72lb

131 BALTOY

Category: Clay Doll
Type: Ground/Psychic
Attacks: Confusion, Harden, Rapid Spin, Mud Slap, Psybeam, Rock Tomb, Selfdestruct, Ancientpower, Sandstorm, Cosmic Power, Explosion
Evolution: >Claydol
Height: 0.5m/1'8"
Weight: 21.5kg/47lb

136 ARMALDO

Category: Plate
Type: Rock/Bug
Attacks: Scratch, Harden, Mud Sport, Water Gun, Metal Claw, Protect, Ancientpower, Fury Cutter, Slash, Rock Blast
Evolution: None
Height: 1.5m/4'11"
Weight: 68.2kg/150lb

132 CLAYDOL

Category: Clay Doll
Type: Ground/Psychic
Attacks: Teleport, Confusion, Harden, Rapid Spin, Mud Slap, Psybeam, Rock Tomb, Selfdestruct, Ancientpower, Sandstom, Hyper Beam, Cosmic Power, Explosion
Evolution: None
Height: 1.5m/4'11"
Weight: 108kg/238lb

137 IGGLYBUFF

Category: Balloon
Type: Normal
Attacks: Sing, Charm, Defence Curl, Pound, Sweet Kiss
Evolution: >Jigglypuff >Wigglytuff
Height: 0.3m/1'0"
Weight: 1kg/2lb

133 LILEEP

Category: Sea Lily
Type: Rock/Grass
Attacks: Astonish, Constrict, Acid, Ingrain, Confuse Ray, Amnesia, Ancientpower, Stockpile, Spit Up, Swallow
Evolution: >Cradily
Height: 1m/3'3"
Weight: 23.8kg/52lb

138 JIGGLYPUFF

Category: Balloon
Type: Normal
Attacks: Sing, Defence Curl, Pound, Disable, Rollout, Doubleslap, Rest, Body Slam, Mimic, Hyper Voice, Double Edge
Evolution: >Wigglytuff
Height: 0.5m/1'8"
Weight: 5.5kg/12lb

134 CRADILY

Category: Barnacle
Type: Rock/Grass
Attacks: Astonish, Constrict, Acid, Ingrain, Confuse Ray, Amnesia, Ancientpower, Stockpile, Spit Up, Swallow
Evolution: None
Height: 1.5m/4'11"
Weight: 60.4/133lb

139 WIGGLYTUFF

Category: Balloon
Type: Normal
Attacks: Sing, Disable, Defence Curl, Doubleslap
Evolution: None
Height: 1m/3'3"
Weight: 12kg/26lb

135 ANORITH

Category: Old Shrimp
Type: Rock/Bug
Attacks: Scratch, Harden, Mud Sport, Water Gun, Metal Claw, Protect, Ancientpower, Fury Cutter, Slash, Rock Blast
Evolution: >Armaldo
Height: 0.7m/2'4"
Weight: 12.5kg/28lb

140 FEEBAS

Category: Fish
Type: Water
Attacks: Splash, Tackle, Flail
Evolution: >Milotic
Height: 0.6m/2'0"
Weight: 7.4kg/16lb

141 MILOTIC

Category: Tender
Type: Water
Attacks: Water Gun, Wrap, Water Sport, Refresh, Water Pulse, Twister, Recover, Rain Dance, Hydro Pump, Attract, Safeguard
Evolution: None
Height: 6.2m/20'4"
Weight: 162kg/357lb

146 SHUPPET

Category: Puppet
Type: Ghost
Attacks: Knock Off, Screech, Night Shade, Curse, Spite, Will-O-Wisp, Faint Attack, Shadow Ball, Snatch, Grudge
Evolution: >Banette
Height: 0.6m/2'0"
Weight: 2.3kg/5lb

142 CASTFORM

Category: Weather
Type: Normal
Attacks: Tackle, Water Gun, Ember, Powder Snow, Rain Dance, Sunny Day, Hail, Weather Ball
Evolution: None
Height: 0.3m/1'0"
Weight: 0.8kg/2lb

147 BANETTE

Category: Marionette
Type: Ghost
Attacks: Knock Off, Screech, Night Shade, Curse, Spite, Will-O-Wisp, Faint Attack, Shadow Ball, Snatch, Grudge
Evolution: None
Height: 1.1m/3'7"
Weight: 12.5kg/28lb

143 STARYU

Category: Star Shape
Type: Water
Attacks: Tackle, Harden, Water Gun, Rapid Spin, Recover, Camouflage, Swift, Bubblebeam, Minimise, Light Screen, Cosmic Power, Hydro Pump
Evolution: >Starmie
Height: 0.8m/2'7"
Weight: 34.5kg/76lb

148 DUSKULL

Category: Requiem
Type: Ghost
Attacks: Leer, Night Shade, Disable, Foresight, Astonish, Confuse Ray, Pursuit, Curse, Will-O-Wisp, Mean Look, Future Sight
Evolution: >Dusclops
Height: 0.8m/2'7"
Weight: 15kg/33lb

144 STARMIE

Category: Mysterious
Type: Water/Psychic
Attacks: Water Gun, Rapid Spin, Recover, Swift, Confuse Ray
Evolution: None
Height: 1.1m/3'7"
Weight: 80kg/176lb

149 DUSCLOPS

Category: Beckon
Type: Ghost
Attacks: Bind, Leer, Night Shade, Disable, Foresight, Astonish, Confuse Ray, Pursuit, Curse, Shadow Punch, Will-O-Wisp, Mean Look, Future Sight
Evolution: None
Height: 1.6m/5'3"
Weight: 30.6kg/67lb

145 KECLEON

Category: Colour Swap
Type: Normal
Attacks: Thief, Tail Whip, Astonish, Lick, Scratch, Bind, Faint Attack, Fury Swipes, Psybeam, Screech, Slash, Substitute, Ancientpower
Evolution: None
Height: 1m/3'3"
Weight: 22kg/49lb

150 TROPIUS

Category: Fruit
Type: Grass/Flying
Attacks: Leer, Gust, Growth, Razor Leaf, Stomp, Sweet Scent, Whirlwind, Magical Leaf, Body Slam, Solarbeam, Synthesis
Evolution: None
Height: 2m/6'7"
Weight: 100kg/221lb

151 CHIMECHO

Category: Wind Chime
Type: Psychic
Attacks: Wrap, Growl, Astonish, Confusion, Take Down, Uproar, Yawn, Psywave, Double Edge, Heal Bell, Safeguard, Psychic
Evolution: None
Height: 0.6m/2'0"
Weight: 1kg/2lb

156 PIKACHU

Category: Mouse
Type: Electric
Attacks: Thundershock, Growl, Tail Whip, Thunder Wave, Quick Attack, Double Team, Slam, Thunderbolt, Agility, Thunder, Light Screen
Evolution: >Raichu
Height: 0.4m/1'4"
Weight: 6kg/13lb

152 ABSOL

Category: Disaster
Type: Dark
Attacks: Scratch, Leer, Taunt, Quick Attack, Razor Wind, Bite, Swords Dance, Double Team, Slash, Future Sight, Perish Song
Evolution: None
Height: 1.2m/3'11"
Weight: 47kg/104lb

157 RAICHU

Category: Mouse
Type: Electric
Attacks: Thundershock, Tail Whip, Quick Attack, Thunderbolt
Evolution: None
Height: 0.8m/2'7"
Weight: 30kg/66lb

153 VULPIX

Category: Fox
Type: Fire
Attacks: Ember, Tail Whip, Roar, Quick Attack, Will-O-Wisp, Confuse Ray, Imprison, Flamethrower, Safeguard, Grudge, Fire Spin
Evolution: >Ninetales
Height: 0.6m/2'0"
Weight: 9.9kg/22lb

158 PSYDUCK

Category: Duck
Type: Water
Attacks: Water Sport, Scratch, Tail Whip, Disable, Confusion, Screech, Psych Up, Fury Swipes, Hydro Pump
Evolution: >Golduck
Height: 0.8m/2'7"
Weight: 19.6kg/43lb

154 NINETALES

Category: Fox
Type: Fire
Attacks: Ember, Quick Attack, Confuse Ray, Safeguard, Fire Spin
Evolution: None
Height: 1.1m/3'7"
Weight: 19.9kg/44lb

159 GOLDUCK

Category: Duck
Type: Water
Attacks: Water Sport, Scratch, Tail Whip, Disable, Confusion, Screech, Psych Up, Fury Swipes, Hydro Pump
Evolution: None
Height: 1.7m/5'7"
Weight: 76.6kg/169lb

155 PICHU

Category: Tiny Mouse
Type: Electric
Attacks: Thundershock, Charm, Tail Whip, Thunder Wave, Sweet Kiss
Evolution: >Pikachu >Raichu
Height: 0.3m/1'0"
Weight: 2kg/4lb

160 WYNAUT

Category: Bright
Type: Psychic
Attacks: Splash, Charm, Encore, Counter, Mirror Coat, Safeguard, Destiny Bond
Evolution: >Wobbuffet
Height: 0.6m/2'0"
Weight: 14kg/31lb

WHICH WAY, MAY?

Can you help May catch up with her friends without running into treacherous Team Rocket?

PIKACHU'S PALS

Pikachu has lots of Pokémon friends! Help them find their shadows

a

b

1

c

2

d

3

4

A POACHED EGO

Ash and his friends were heading for Rustboro City, where Ash would have his first gym battle in the Hoenn Region.
Max pulled out his Pokémon Navigator.
"There's a Pokémon Centre just ahead!"
May slipped and fell against a tree.
"Ow!" she cried. "There's something weird sticking out of this tree!"
"What is it?" wondered Ash, pulling the strange object out of the tree trunk.
"Pika!" cried Pikachu. Bark had been torn from all the trees around them!
"Something sure happened here!" said Brock.

When they arrived at the Pokémon Centre, they found Officer Jenny talking to Nurse Joy.
"Have any injured Pokémon have been brought here?" she said.
"No," replied Nurse Joy. "Why do you ask?

"There have been reports of a poacher in this area!" explained Officer Jenny, showing them a picture. "We think it's this Pokémon hunter, Rico. He injures Pokémon in order to catch them!"
"We found this in the forest!" said Ash, pulling the strange object out and showing it to Officer Jenny.
"That's part of a capture net!" she exclaimed. "You must show me exactly where it was!"

WANTED

Team Rocket was thinking up a new plan to catch Pikachu when they saw something very strange. It was a huge cage – full of Ekans!
"What are you guys doing in there?" Meowth exclaimed.
The Ekans told Meowth that a poacher had captured them. But when Meowth tried to open the cage, it gave him an electric shock!
"The electricity in the cage has zapped the Ekans pretty badly!" said Meowth.
"What kind of idiots would injure their own Pokémon?" Jessie frowned.

Arbok was crying!

"Arbok used to be an Ekans before it evolved!" realised Meowth. "It doesn't want them to be hurt!"

Arbok launched its Acid Attack – but it had no effect on the cage!

"Weezing!" cried James. "Use Sludge Attack!"

But that was just as useless! Then a man drove up. It was Rico the poacher with his Fearow Pokémon!

"What do you think you're doing with my Pokémon?" he demanded.

"Stealing them, of course!" laughed Jessie.

"You don't know who you're dealing with!" Rico growled.

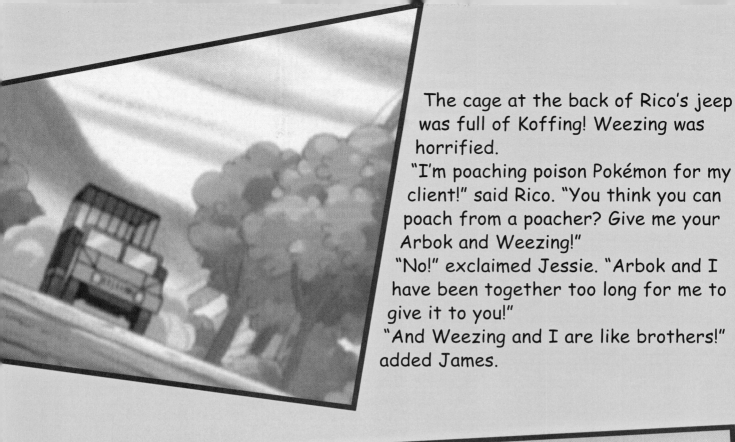

The cage at the back of Rico's jeep was full of Koffing! Weezing was horrified.

"I'm poaching poison Pokémon for my client!" said Rico. "You think you can poach from a poacher? Give me your Arbok and Weezing!"

"No!" exclaimed Jessie. "Arbok and I have been together too long for me to give it to you!"

"And Weezing and I are like brothers!" added James.

"Fine – I'll just have to take them!" snarled Rico. "Fearow – Agility – GO!"
Fearow swooped down on Team Rocket.
"Arbok – Poison Sting!" yelled Jessie.
"Weezing – Sludge Attack!" cried James.
Fearow tried to fight back, but Arbok used Wrap Attack. Fearow was defeated!
"Fearow – return!" called Rico. "Pupitar – Sandstorm!"
Team Rocket was blasted into the distance!

Ash showed Officer Jenny where they had found the piece of net.
Max noticed a set of tyre tracks leading away from the trees.
"The poachers must be travelling by car," said Officer Jenny.
"We'll search from the sky!" said Ash, releasing Taillow.

Team Rocket was attacked by a group of Beedrill. But a Cacnea appeared and drove them away!

"Thanks!" gasped James. "You really saved our skins!"

"I say we find that poacher and save Ekans and Koffing!" Jessie suggested.

Arbok put his head to the ground to listen for the sound of the poacher's jeep.

The Cacnea was still hopping around James' feet.

"Have these," smiled James, giving it a bag of cookies. "A 'thank you' present!"

Arbok picked up on the poacher's jeep and Team Rocket sped off, leaving the Cacnea behind.

Taillow was also searching for Rico. At last it spotted him.
"Tail-low!" it called to Ash.
"Lead us to him!" Ash replied.

Arbok blocked Rico's jeep and Weezing used Smokescreen to blind him!
"How dare you!" spluttered Rico. "Fearow – blow Smokescreen away!"
Meowth was picking the lock of the cage. The electricity wasn't bothering him!
"This is nothing compared to Pikachu's Thunderbolt!" laughed Meowth. The cage door swung open and the Ekans and Koffing escaped!
"No you don't!" screamed Rico, pulling out a gun. Arbok knocked it from his hand.
"You've poached your last Pokémon!" James laughed. "These Ekans and Koffing are coming with us!"

"You've done it now!" yelled Rico. "GO – Pupitar!"
Pupitar started to evolve!
"Tyranitar!" screamed James.
"Wow – that's a big one!" said Meowth.
"Big deal!" sneered Jessie. "A Hyper Beam ought to teach him a lesson – Wobbuffet – GO!"
But before Wobbuffet could attack, Tyranitar blasted Team Rocket with Hyper Beam!
"What was that?" exclaimed Ash, seeing the explosion in the distance.
"I bet it's that poacher again!" said Brock. "Come on!"

"I'm going to destroy you!" Rico yelled.

"Arbok," said Jessie quietly, "take your friends and get out of here..."

"You too, Weezing," said James. "You're no match for Tyranitar."

But Arbok and Weezing shook their heads.

"Listen!" said Jessie desperately. "We care too much to allow you to be captured by someone like him! Besides – all those Ekans and Koffing need you to help them!"

"You guys get outta here and don't look back!" added Meowth.

Unwillingly, Arbok and Weezing disappeared into the forest with the Ekans and Koffing.

"Idiots!" jeered Rico. "They're not going anywhere! Tyranitar – Hyper Beam!"
"Fury Swipes!" shouted Meowth, launching itself at Tyranitar.
"Try my Fury Swipes!" yelled Jessie, hurling herself forward.
"And mine!" cried James, doing the same.
Team Rocket fought bravely, but they were no match for the mighty
Tyranitar! Rico laughed as he looked at them lying on the ground.
"Now those Pokémon are mine – but where did they go?"

When Rico entered the forest, Officer Jenny was waiting for him!

"You're under arrest for Pokémon poaching!" she said.

"Is that so? Fearow – GO!" Rico snarled.

"Pikachu! Use Thunderbolt!" yelled Ash. Fearow was knocked out.

"Growlithe! Seize his Poké Balls' now!" cried Officer Jenny. Before Rico could use Tyranitar, his Poké Balls' were gone!

"Now, she said, "release all the Pokémon you've caught!"

"You're too late," growled Rico. "They escaped – thanks to a bunch of fools!"

"That must have been the explosion we saw!" said May.

"With all the bad people like Team Rocket around, it's nice to know there are good people too!" Ash smiled.

Team Rocket was miserable.

"Do you think Arbok and Weezing'll be all right?" asked James.

"I hope so..." Jessie replied.

"Don't worry, guys!" said Meowth. "They're as tough as nails from all that battling with Pikachu, right? They'll be just fine!"

"I suppose..." said James. Then he gave a cry. The Cacnea they met earlier was right behind them – and it still had the bag of cookies!

"Have you been following us all this time?" James asked. Cacnea nodded.

"You can eat these cookies! I have them for you!"

James fed Cacnea with one of the cookies.

"It's kinda cute!" admitted Meowth.

"Cacnea," said James, "would you like to travel with us?"

Cacnea said yes! James and Jessie started to feel better. Saying goodbye to Arbok and Weezing had been tough, but now it was time to discover brand new Pokémon in the Hoenn Region!

161 WOBBUFFET

Category: Patient
Type: Psychic
Attacks: Counter, Mirror Coat, Safeguard, Destiny Bond
Evolution: None
Height: 1.3m/4'3"
Weight: 28.5kg/63lb

166 DONPHAN

Category: Armour
Type: Ground
Attacks: Odour Sleuth, Horn Attack, Growl, Defence Curl, Flail, Fury Attack, Rollout, Rapid Spin, Earthquake
Evolution: None
Height: 1.1m/3'7"
Weight: 120kg/265lb

162 NATU

Category: Tiny Bird
Type: Psychic/Flying
Attacks: Peck, Leer, Night Shade, Teleport, Wish, Future Sight, Confuse Ray, Psychic
Evolution: >Xatu
Height: 0.2m/0'8"
Weight: 2kg/4lb

167 PINSIR

Category: Stag Beetle
Type: Bug
Attacks: Vicegrip, Focus Energy, Bind, Seismic Toss, Harden, Revenge, Brick Break, Guillotine, Submission, Swords Dance
Evolution: None
Height: 1.5m/4'11"
Weight: 55kg/121lb

163 XATU

Category: Mystic
Type: Psychic/Flying
Attacks: Peck, Leer, Night Shade, Teleport, Wish, Future Sight, Confuse Ray, Psychic
Evolution: None
Height: 1.5m/4'11"
Weight: 15kg/33lb

168 HERACROSS

Category: Single Horn
Type: Bug/Fighting
Attacks: Tackle, Leer, Horn Attack, Endure, Fury Attack, Brick Break, Counter, Take Down, Reversal, Megahorn
Evolution: None
Height: 1.5m/4'11"
Weight: 54kg/119lb

164 GIRAFARIG

Category: Long Neck
Type: Normal/Psychic
Attacks: Tackle, Growl, Astonish, Confusion, Stomp, Odour Sleuth, Agility, Baton Pass, Psybeam, Crunch
Evolution: None
Height: 1.5m/4'11"
Weight: 41.5kg/92lb

169 RHYHORN

Category: Spikes
Type: Ground/Rock
Attacks: Horn Attack, Tail Whip, Stomp, Fury Attack, Scary Face, Rock Blast, Horn Drill, Take Down, Earthquake, Megahorn
Evolution: >Rhydon
Height: 1m/3'3"
Weight: 115kg/254lb

165 PHANPY

Category: Long Nose
Type: Ground
Attacks: Odour Sleuth, Tackle, Growl, Defence Curl, Flail, Take Down, Rollout, Endure, Double Edge
Evolution: >Donphan
Height: 0.5m/1'8"
Weight: 33.5kg/74lb

170 RHYDON

Category: Drill
Type: Ground/Rock
Attacks: Horn Attack, Tail Whip, Stomp, Fury Attack, Scary Face, Rock Blast, Horn Drill, Take Down Earthquake, Megahorn
Evolution: None
Height: 1.9m/6'3"
Weight: 120kg/265lb

171 SNORUNT

Category: Snow Hat
Type: Ice
Attacks: Powder Snow, Leer, Double Team, Bite, Icy Wind, Headbutt, Protect, Crunch, Ice Beam, Hail, Blizzard
Evolution: >Glalie
Height: 0.7m/2'4"
Weight: 16.8kg/37lb

176 CLAMPERL

Category: Bivalve
Type: Water
Attacks: Clamp, Water Gun, Whirlpool, Iron Defence
Evolution: >Huntail >Gorebyss
Height: 0.4m/1'4"
Weight: 52.5/116lb

172 GLALIE

Category: Face
Type: Ice
Attacks: Powder Snow, Leer, Double Team, Bite, Icy Wind, Headbutt, Protect, Crunch, Ice Beam, Hail, Blizzard, Sheer Cold
Evolution: None
Height: 1.5m/4'11"
Weight: 256.5kg/566lb

177 HUNTAIL

Category: Deep Sea
Type: Water
Attacks: Whirlpool, Bite, Screech, Water Pulse, Scary Face, Crunch, Baton Pass, Hydro Pump
Evolution: >Gorebyss
Height: 1.7m/5'7"
Weight: 27kg/60lb

173 SPHEAL

Category: Clap
Type: Ice/Water
Attacks: Powder Snow, Growl, Water Gun, Encore, Ice Ball, Body Slam, Aurora Beam, Hail, Rest, Snore, Blizzard, Sheer Cold
Evolution: >Sealeo >Walrein
Height: 0.8m/2'7"
Weight: 39.5kg/87lb

178 GOREBYSS

Category: South Sea
Type: Water
Attacks: Whirlpool, Confusion, Agility, Water Pulse, Amnesia, Psychic, Baton Pass, Hydro Pump
Evolution: None
Height: 1.8m/5'11"
Weight: 22.6kg/50lb

174 SEALEO

Category: Ball Roll
Type: Ice/Water
Attacks: Powder Snow, Growl, Water Gun, Encore, Ice Ball, Body Slam, Aurora Beam, Hail, Rest, Snore, Blizzard, Sheer Cold
Evolution: >Walrein
Height: 1.1m/3'7"
Weight: 87.6kg/193lb

179 RELICANTH

Category: Longevity
Type: Water/Rock
Attacks: Tackle, Harden, Water Gun, Rock Tomb, Yawn, Take Down, Mud Sport, Ancientpower, Rest, Double Edge, Hydro Pump
Evolution: None
Height: 1m/3'3"
Weight: 23.4kg/52lb

175 WALREIN

Category: Ice Break
Type: Ice/Water
Attacks: Powder Snow, Growl, Water Gun, Encore, Ice Ball, Body Slam, Aurora Beam, Hail, Rest, Snore, Blizzard, Sheer Cold
Evolution: None
Height: 1.4m/4'7"
Weight: 150.6kg/332lb

180 CORSOLA

Category: Coral
Type: Water/Rock
Attacks: Tackle, Harden, Bubble, Recover, Refresh, Bubblebeam, Spike Cannon, Rock Blast, Mirror Coat, Ancientpower
Evolution: None
Height: 0.6m/2'0"
Weight: 5kg/11lb

181 CHINCHOU

Category: Angler
Type: Water/Electric
Attacks: Bubble, Thunder Wave, Supersonic, Flail, Water Gun, Spark, Confuse Ray, Take Down, Hydro Pump, Charge
Evolution: >Lanturn
Height: 0.5m/1'8"
Weight: 12kg/26lb

186 KINGDRA

Category: Dragon
Type: Water/Dragon
Attacks: Bubble, Smokescreen, Leer, Water Gun, Twister, Agility, Hydro Pump, Dragon Dance
Evolution: None
Height: 1.8m/5'11"
Weight: 152kg/335lb

182 LANTURN

Category: Light
Type: Water/Electric
Attacks: Bubble, Thunder Wave, Supersonic, Flail, Water Gun, Spark, Confuse Ray, Take Down, Hydro Pump, Charge
Evolution: None
Height: 1.2m3'11"
Weight: 22.5kg/50lb

187 BAGON

Category: Rock Head
Type: Dragon
Attacks: Rage, Bite, Leer, Headbutt, Focus Energy, Ember, Dragonbreath, Scary Face, Crunch Dragon Claw, Double Edge
Evolution: >Shelgon >Salamence
Height: 0.6m/2'0"
Weight: 42.1kg/93lb

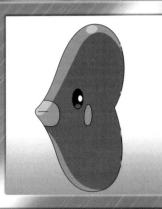

183 LUVDISC

Category: Rendezvous
Type: Water
Attacks: Tackle, Charm, Water Gun, Agility, Take Down, Sweet Kiss, Attract, Flail, Safeguard
Evolution: None
Height: 0.6m/2'0"
Weight: 8.7kg/19lb

188 SHELGON

Category: Endurance
Type: Dragon
Attacks: Rage, Bite, Leer, Headbutt, Focus Energy, Ember, Protect, Dragonbreath, Scary Face, Crunch, Dragon Claw, Double Edge
Evolution: >Salamence
Height: 1.1m/3'7"
Weight: 110.5kg/244lb

184 HORSEA

Category: Dragon
Type: Water
Attacks: Bubble, Smokescreen, Leer, Water Gun, Twister, Agility, Hydro Pump, Dragon Dance
Evolution: >Seadra >Kingdra
Height: 0.4m/1'4"
Weight: 8kg/18lb

189 SALAMENCE

Category: Dragon
Type: Dragon/Flying
Attacks: Rage, Bite, Leer, Headbutt, Focus Energy, Ember, Protect, Dragonbreath, Scary Face, Fly, Crunch, Dragon Claw, Double Edge
Evolution: None
Height: 1.5m/4'11"
Weight: 102.6kg/226lb

185 SEADRA

Category: Dragon
Type: Water
Attacks: Bubble, Smokescreen, Leer, Water Gun, Twister, Agility, Hydro Pump, Dragon Dance
Evolution: >Kingdra
Height: 1.2m/3'11"
Weight: 25kg/55lb

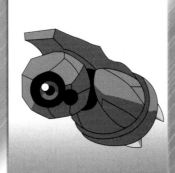

190 BELDUM

Category: Iron Ball
Type: Steel/Psychic
Attacks: Take Down
Evolution: >Metang >Metagross
Height: 0.6m/2'0"
Weight: 95.2kg/210lb

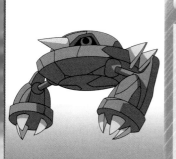

191 METANG

Category: Iron Claw
Type: Steel/Psychic
Attacks: Take Down, Confusion, Metal Claw, Scary Face, Pursuit, Psychic, Iron Defence, Meteor Mash, Agiliity, Hyper Beam
Evolution: >Metagross
Height: 1.2m/3'11"
Weight: 202.5kg/447

196 LATIAS

Category: Eon
Type: Dragon/Psychic
Attacks: Psywave, Wish, Helping Hand, Safeguard, Dragonbreath, Water Sport, Refresh, Mist Ball, Psychic, Recover, Charm
Evolution: None
Height: 1.4m/4'7"
Weight: 40kg/88lb

192 METAGROSS

Category: Iron Leg
Type: Steel/Psychic
Attacks: Take Down, Confusion, Metal Claw, Scary Face, Pursuit, Psychic, Iron Defence, Meteor Mash, Agiliity, Hyper Beam
Evolution: None
Height: 1.6m/5'3"
Weight: 550kg/1213lb

197 LATIOS

Category: Eon
Type: Dragon/Psychic
Attacks: Psywave, Memento, Helping Hand, Safeguard, Dragonbreath, Protect, Refresh, Luster Purge, Psychic, Recover, Dragon Dance
Evolution: None
Height: 2m/6'7"
Weight: 60kg/132lb

193 REGIROCK

Category: Rock Peak
Type: Rock
Attacks: Explosion, Rock Throw, Curse, Superpower, Ancientpower, Iron Defence, Zap Cannon, Lock On, Hyper Beam
Evolution: None
Height: 1.7m/5'7"
Weight: 230kg/507

198 KYOGRE

Category: Sea Basin
Type: Water
Attacks: Water Pulse, Scary Face, Ancientpower, Body Slam, Calm Mind, Ice Beam, Hydro Pump, Rest, Sheer Cold, Double Edge, Water Spout
Evolution: None
Height: 4.5m/14'9"
Weight: 352kg/776lb

194 REGICE

Category: Iceberg
Type: Ice
Attacks: Explosion, Icy Wind, Curse, Superpower, Ancientpower, Amnesia, Zap Cannon, Lock On, Hyper Beam
Evolution: None
Height: 1.8m/5'11"
Weight: 175kg/386lb

199 GROUDON

Category: Continent
Type: Ground
Attacks: Mud Shot, Scary Face, Ancientpower, Slash, Bulk Up, Earthquake, Fire Blast, Rest, Fissure. Solarbeam, Eruption
Evolution: None
Height: 3.5m/11'6"
Weight: 950kg/2095lb

195 REGISTEEL

Category: Iron
Type: Steel
Attacks: Explosion, Metal Claw, Curse, Superpower, Ancientpower, Iron Defence, Amnesia, Zap Cannon, Lock On, Hyper Beam
Evolution: None
Height: 1.9m/6'3"
Weight: 205kg/452lb

200 RAYQUAZA

Category: Sky High
Type: Dragon/Flying
Attacks: Twister, Scary Face, Ancientpower, Dragon Claw, Dragon Dance, Crunch, Fly, Rest, Extremespeed, Outrage, Hyper Beam
Evolution: None
Height: 7m/23'0"
Weight: 206.5kg/455lb

ANSWERS

Page 12:

Mudkip evolves to Marshtomp
Torchic evolves to Combusken
Cacnea evolves to Cacturne
Azurill evolves to Marill
Jigglypuff evolves to Wigglytuff

Page 87:

Pikachu's Pals are Luvdisc, Clamperl,
Kecleon and Whiscash